Auntie and Other Aliens

Written by
Douglas Hill

Illustrated by Neil Chapman,
Chris Pepper and
Lorenzo van der Lingen

Contents

Auntie Madge...4

Deserted Planet...................................29

The Chetty 55

Auntie Madge

When I crashed into the football goalpost, it knocked me out. And when I came round, I felt shaky and sick, my head really hurt, and I was seeing flashing lights that weren't really there.

But the next day I found that I could see something else. And only *I* could see it. It wasn't anything that I wanted to see. Because it was about as scary as you can get.

That morning my aching head had a cut and bump, and my mum thought I might have something called concussion. So I was in bed, half-dozing, when the door opened.

'Peter, dear,' Mum said. 'Here's your Auntie Madge come to see you. She's staying with us for a while.'

I was wide awake in a hurry. I had three aunties – none of them called Madge. And none of them was *anything* like this one.

She was short and skinny with pale hair, wearing a long robe down to her ankles. Her skin was grey-white, and she had a pinched mouth and shiny eyes that never blinked.

'Hello, Peter,' she said, in a stiff, flat voice. 'I am sorry you are not well.'

I just stared. It must be me, I thought, with my sore head, not seeing straight or thinking straight, because Mum was smiling as if it was normal to have a weird stranger in the house pretending to be an aunt.

'Say hello to your auntie, dear,' Mum smiled.

I was still staring, not knowing what to do. 'H'lo,' I mumbled.

'He'll be brighter when his head's better,' Mum said, and they went out – the Madge person walking just as stiffly as she talked.

Throughout that day I kept trying to ask Mum about Auntie Madge, but I never seemed to get her on her own. Then next morning I was feeling better, so I got up early. I wasn't going to spend the summer holiday in bed, and I was sort of half-hoping that Auntie Madge had been some kind of bad dream.

But though I was wide awake and my headache had gone, she was still there –

having breakfast with Mum and Dad, and looking just as strange and scary as before.

She didn't eat or drink much, and was clumsy with spoons and cups. She didn't talk much, either, and gazed around as if she'd never seen a kitchen before. And all the while Mum and Dad chatted happily, as if they were having breakfast with a normal visitor. I still felt completely stunned, with no idea what was happening or what to do. But I didn't want to hang around Auntie Madge any more than I had to, so I went to see the twins.

He's Alan and she's Nala (Alan spelt backwards). They go to the same school as me, they live down the street, and they're my best friends. Even though, that day, they teased me about hitting the goalpost, then laughed when I told them about Auntie Madge.

'That bump on your head's making you see things!' Nala giggled.

'It's funny, though,' Alan said. 'Our Uncle George is visiting us.'

I felt suddenly cold. 'What's he like?' I asked, just as the twins' dad came into the room – with a stranger.

'Hello, Peter,' their dad said cheerily. 'This is the twins' Uncle George, from Trinidad.'

That's where the twins' grandparents came from. But the stranger didn't look anything like any of them. He was short and bony, in a long robe, with pale hair and shiny eyes and grey-white skin – just like Auntie Madge.

'Hello, Peter,' he said, in the same flat voice. Alan, Nala and their dad smiled and no one saw anything wrong at all.

It's only me, I thought. I'm the only one who can *see* what they really are ...

Then it came to me. It was probably because I had bumped my head. And that gave me an idea – something I didn't want to do, but had to ...

When we wandered out into their garden, with no one around to see, I got behind the twins, grabbed them, and banged their heads together.

I'd caught them by surprise, so it really hurt them. Alan yelled and staggered, Nala nearly fell over – then they turned on me, furious.

'What did you do that for?' they screamed.

'So you'd *see*,' I said, backing off. 'I'm sorry, but I had to. Come back in and look at Uncle George again – and then you can bash *me*, if you still want to.'

Alan seemed ready to have a go right then, but Nala stopped. 'Wait,' she said. 'Now I think about it, I've never *heard* of any Uncle George.'

That stopped Alan, too. So all three of us, with our sore heads, went back inside the house.

And they saw.

The Uncle George person was in the kitchen with the twins' mum and dad, staring around the way Auntie Madge did. But he didn't look at us – just as well, the way the twins were goggling at him.

We crept away into the hall. 'He looked so *ordinary* before,' Nala gasped.

'Why couldn't we *see* what he really looked like?' Alan asked. 'Why can't Mum and Dad?'

'I don't know,' I said.

'Let's get out of here,' Nala said. So she told her mum that we were going over to my place, and we left.

We live in a village where people know each other. All the kids go to the same school, and everything is mostly quiet and normal. But not that day.

Almost everywhere we looked, we saw more of them. Small, strange people in robes, moving stiffly – and walking with some of the ordinary people of the village. I saw the vicar and his wife with one of them, our school's deputy head with another, and there was even one

with a crowd of teenagers on the green.
No one seemed to notice anything
strange about them.

'We're the only ones who can really
see them,' Alan whispered.

'Don't let on,' I said. 'There's no
telling what they'd do, if they knew.'

We shivered, even though it was a
warm day.

'What *are* they?' Nala asked.

'They seem to be some sort of …
alien people,' Alan said, 'with the power
to hide what they look like.'

I nodded. 'Like putting a spell on
people. And being hit on the head
breaks the spell.'

'We have to *tell* someone,' Nala said.
'The police, or something.'

'They wouldn't believe us, because of
the spell,' Alan told her.

'I'm not hitting any policemen on the
head,' I muttered.

'I wonder if they're just here,' Nala
whispered, 'or all over the world.'

That made us shiver again. 'Let's go
to my house,' I said. 'If they're
everywhere, there should be some of
them on TV.'

When we got to my house, Dad had
gone to work, but Mum was in the
garden – with Auntie Madge.

I switched on the TV, but there was
no sign of any of the strange beings on
any channel. Not even when the news
showed a lot of crowded streets in
different cities.

'They must be just here in the village,' Alan said.

'But what would they want *here*?' Nala asked.

'We could find out,' I said. 'We could spy on them. We might find a way to break the spell. But we'd have to be careful not to show that we ...'

Then Nala gasped, and I spun around. Auntie Madge was standing in the doorway, staring at us.

Mum bustled past her. 'Hello, you lot,' she said. 'Why are you watching TV on such a lovely day?'

'Just ... um ... looking for a football score,' I mumbled.

And all the while Auntie Madge stared and stared. As if she'd heard. As if she knew that we knew ...

She went on watching me the next morning, which made me really nervous. But Mum had chores for me, so I couldn't get away from those shiny eyes.

Then in the afternoon, when I was in the living room, Auntie Madge went stiffly past the door, down the hall, and out of the house.

Without stopping to think, I went after her. I kept well back, ready to dodge behind a bush or a car if she looked around. But she never did. She just stalked along the street – to the twins' house.

The door was opened before she reached it – by Uncle George, and they set off together along the street.

And through the door behind them came Alan and Nala, who jumped when they saw me.

'Did you follow Auntie Madge?' Nala said.

I nodded. 'It wasn't hard. She didn't

look round once.'

'Come on,' Alan said. 'We don't want to lose them.'

We probably could have walked right behind them, as they both looked straight ahead all the time. They didn't speak, either. They just went along in their stiff-legged way to the edge of the village, then on to a lane through a patch of woods.

We hung back, nervous about following them into the woods, but then they turned off the lane and went through the gate of the McKinney place.

The big old rambling house was covered with overgrown ivy, most of its windows boarded up. It once belonged to a rich family, but has been empty for years. Some people say it's haunted, and it looks creepy enough. Right then, it was even creepier.

Crouching among the bushes, we watched Auntie Madge and Uncle George go into the old house. Then everything grew still again, except for a deep humming sound that seemed a long way away.

'What are they *doing* in there?' Alan
wondered.

I took a deep breath. 'We could sneak
up and look through a window.'

The twins nodded and we moved

away through the woods. We headed for the side of the house, where bushes grew almost up to one of the windows. At last we were within a few feet of the window, even more scared, getting ready to take the risk of looking in. I was sure the thumping of my heart could be heard for miles.

And that was when the weird people in robes appeared out of the bushes all around, and grabbed us.

There were six of them – two for each of us. Though they were all short and skinny and awkward, they were strong, lifting us up as if we were light as feathers. Silently, they carried us inside, into a hallway with doors on either side and stairs ahead, everything dusty and dirty and rundown.

Then they took us through one doorway into a huge room – to face Auntie Madge.

She was standing in the centre, with Uncle George beside her, as if they were the *leaders*. There were more of the beings crowded behind.

'You three can see the truth of us,'
Auntie Madge said in her flat voice.
'*How*?'

But our throats were closed up with
fear, and none of us said anything.

'Speak!' Uncle George ordered. 'Why
does the mind-veil not work on you?'

'W-what's a mind-veil?' I stammered.

Auntie Madge waved a bony hand towards a square of dark metal fixed to one of the peeling walls. 'That device affects the minds of all the humans in this area, so they see us as humans too, and as members of their families.'

'Then you're ...' Alan began.

'We are from another world,' Uncle George said.

'And somehow *you* see us truly,' Auntie Madge said, her eyes flashing. '*Explain*!'

'We ... we hit our heads,' I mumbled.

Auntie Madge twitched. 'So,' she said, 'sudden brain-shock. Just a simple mischance.'

'And no others seem unveiled,' Uncle George said. 'So we are safe. And the work is nearly done.'

'What work?' I asked, before I could stop myself.

Auntie Madge ignored me. 'Lock them away on the upper level,' she ordered. 'We will deal with them at the end.'

'What are you going to do to us?' Nala whispered.

'We will make sure,' Uncle George said flatly, 'that you can never tell *anyone* what you have seen.'

The words turned me icy cold. 'You *can't* ...!' I yelled. But we were carried out and up the stairs, kicking and struggling, shoved into a bare, dark room, and the door was locked.

We nearly started screaming in panic. We were trapped. The door was locked, the walls looked solid, and boards covered the window, blocking it up completely.

But we were saved from panic by a sudden noise – a rattle, coming from the window.

Nala went to look. Then, to our surprise, she laughed.

'It's not boarded up!' she cried. 'These are *shutters*, with a latch.'

The latch was old and rusty, but we tugged and wiggled it and got it open. Then we heaved at the shutters till they swung apart – to reveal a tall window,

mostly broken, and a balcony beyond it.

'Why would they put us here,' Alan asked, 'when it's so easy to get out?'

'They're aliens,' Nala said. 'They probably don't know about shutters and thought the window was boarded up.'

'Come on,' I said, poking at the broken glass in the window frame.

In a minute we had cleared a space big enough to crawl through safely. And the huge old ivy growing up the wall beside the balcony was as good as a ladder. In another minute we were on the ground, behind a bush at the side of the house.

We couldn't see any aliens, and we couldn't hear anything except the strange faraway humming, so we crept towards the back of the house where the trees and bushes grew more thickly, to hide us as we escaped.

And we nearly died of shock when we heard the yell.

Ahead of us, above the trees, we saw a high metal platform, held up by three tall metal legs. A long pipe, attached to the platform, was sticking into the ground, and there was strange machinery around it. Two aliens were perched on the platform as well, pointing down at us, yelling strange words.

We ran in terror, hearing aliens yelling and crashing through the trees and bushes around us – until in a moment we burst out into an open area in the middle of the old house's huge garden. The three legs of the high platform stood in front of us, with more machinery all around. But we didn't stop. A crowd of aliens rushed out of the trees behind us, and we raced away, towards the tall metal legs.

I was slightly ahead of the twins as we reached the alien machines. And then I wasn't running any more.

I was falling – into a pit I hadn't seen.

In that instant, I took in everything at once. The pit was only a few metres across – a perfect circle with smooth sides. But it was terrifyingly deep. Down and down into utter blackness, with a glow at the bottom, like dark-red flame.

As I fell, I opened my mouth to scream. But I only gasped, with another shock.

The air was filled with a loud humming – the sound we'd heard before, but much closer. And something invisible took hold of me, and stopped my fall.

For a horrible moment I hung there, over the pit. Then an invisible force swung me up and set me down beside the pit, below the three metal legs.

Alan and Nala stood there staring, grey with fright. A mass of aliens in a circle stood all around, and Auntie Madge and Uncle George moved stiffly towards us.

'Please ... don't hurt us,' Nala

whispered.

The crowd of aliens stirred, with a sound like an angry growl. Then Auntie Madge raised her hands as if to grab us – but instead she totally amazed us.

'*Hurt* you?' she said, looking shocked, her hands fluttering. 'We could not do that!'

'Did we not catch you, with the magni-hoist?' Uncle George said to me. 'We could not let you fall.'

'Our people *cannot* harm living creatures,' Auntie Madge said. All the aliens growled again, as if agreeing. 'It is our world's oldest decree.'

'That is why we used the mind-veil,' Uncle George said. 'So your people would not fear us. If they attacked us, we would not be able to defend ourselves.'

'Then why are you here?' Alan asked.

'To seek a rare mineral,' Auntie Madge said, 'found in the core of some planets. The mineral helps to power our spaceship. If we had not found it here, far below this place, our ship would have failed.'

'There is only enough power to keep it in orbit,' Uncle George said. 'None to provide air, or food. That is why we had to come among you humans.'

'So you've been *digging*,' Nala murmured, 'to the centre of the earth.'

'Yes,' said Auntie Madge. 'We have the mineral now and our ship is restored. We will leave after we have made this place as it was, and after the mind-veil allows you humans to forget us.'

'Is *that* what you meant?' I burst out. 'When you said you'd make sure that we never tell anyone about you?'

'We thought you meant you'd *kill* us,' Alan said.

Auntie Madge looked horrified. '*Never*,' she said. 'The mind-veil simply

erases memories.'

'Do you *have* to erase our memories?' Nala asked.

'Couldn't you let us remember?' pleaded Alan.

'We'd never tell,' I said.

Uncle George looked at Auntie Madge. 'They deserve something after being so frightened,' he said.

'Very well,' Auntie Madge decided. 'You three may keep your memories of this adventure. But keep them to yourselves.'

'We promise!' the twins said.

'No one would believe us anyway,' I muttered.

So we were allowed to watch while the aliens packed away the platform with its tall legs, where they had been drilling into the earth. Then, with other machines, they put the old garden back just the way it was.

At last, all the aliens and their machines clustered together. 'Farewell,' Auntie Madge said. 'It has been pleasant meeting you.'

We barely had time to say goodbye. A huge glowing bubble dropped from the sky, settled over the aliens, then rose again, carrying them back to their ship.

Since then we've kept our promise not to tell, but it has been hard keeping the secret. We've never stopped *wanting* to tell. And now, a few years later, I've had the idea of telling it as a *story* – a piece of fiction. So I'm not really giving the secret away, because no one reading this story would ever believe it really happened. Would they?

Deserted Planet

When the distant planet Ravalle came into view through the starship's long-range scanner, young Kelsey was amazed.

'It looks completely dead,' she said.

'Not dead,' her father said. 'There's plenty of life.'

'Just no alien people any more,' her mother murmured.

'But where could they all have gone?' asked Cale, the ship's computer expert.

The four of them made a very small crew for such an enormous explorer starship. And Kelsey, only ten years old, was just along for the ride. But small crews were normal in Earth's Space Exploration Service. Banks of computers and nearly two hundred robots did the work of operating the ship – so exploring, looking at alien worlds, didn't need many people.

Kelsey's father, Eldron, and her mother, Lurah, were experts on almost everything to do with alien life. Cale looked after all the ship's computer systems and robots.

All four of them were in the control room, looking at the long-range scanner, and its puzzling views of the planet Ravalle.

Although Earth Central had known about Ravalle and its alien population for some time, they hadn't landed a ship to make contact – and now it seemed too late. The aliens of Ravalle, every one of them, had vanished.

A passing freighter-ship from Earth, taking a scanner look at Ravalle, had reported that the planet looked deserted. So, because Eldron's explorer starship was closest, Earth Central had sent him to have a look.

'The alien people couldn't *leave*,' Cale said. 'They don't have space flight.'

'Do you think they all died from some disease?' Kelsey asked.

'The scanner doesn't show any killer germs,' Eldron said. 'But we'll get a better look when we're closer.'

So Kelsey watched the screens until, at last, the starship swooped down into orbit around Ravalle.

The planet seemed to be mostly water, with groups of islands. One big island showed many signs of civilisation, including a large city near a mountain

range. But although the scanner showed plenty of creatures and plants on the planet, there were no alien people anywhere.

'Spooky,' Kelsey said.

'What's that, up in the mountains?' Eldron asked, pointing at the screen.

Cale enlarged the image. 'It's some sort of big square stone building!' he said. 'There's nothing in the databanks about that.'

'Maybe it's new,' Lurah said. 'What's inside?'

'It's too thick for the scanner to see through,' Cale said.

'Strange,' Eldron muttered. 'Let's go down for a look. Cale, will you stay with the starship?'

'Fine,' Cale agreed, always more interested in his machines than aliens.

'Can I come?' Kelsey begged.

Lurah looked at Eldron and he nodded. 'We shouldn't run into trouble on a deserted planet.'

'And the air's good down there,' Lurah said, 'like Earth.'

'We'll wear our shield-suits anyway,' Eldron decided.

Once the three of them had pulled on their tough lightweight suits, they climbed into their small shuttle-ship, flashed down towards the alien mountains, and touched down on a wide flat expanse of rock beside the mysterious building.

They climbed out into strange-smelling alien air – and silence.

'Let's see if this place has a door,' Eldron said quietly.

As they started walking around the building, they came to a tightly closed door. Above it was a narrow slit, with a long shiny cylinder sticking out.

'I think that's some kind of old-style telescope ...' Eldron began.

Suddenly, the door flew open and out stalked a troop of nine alien beings. They were more or less human-shaped, but very tall, with blue hairless skin and shiny round eyes. They all wore strange uniforms and carried long slim objects – which they pointed, like weapons, at the humans.

'Stand where you are!' shouted one of the aliens.

A tiny word-wizard computer in the helmets of the humans instantly translated the alien words. 'We are peaceful visitors ...' Eldron began, and his word-wizard translated the words, through his helmet speaker, into the alien language.

'Silence!' the alien shouted. 'You will explain yourselves to the Ruler!'

With weapons ready, they herded the three humans through the door, past the telescope, then along a corridor to a ramp, which sloped steeply downward for a very long way into echoing darkness.

When they finally reached the bottom, they stared in amazement.

'It's an underground city!' Kelsey gasped.

It looked like the depths of the mountain had been hollowed out, making a gigantic cavern that held a vast array of buildings, with crowds of aliens swarming everywhere.

'Is *this* where all your people are?'
Kelsey asked the alien nearest her.

'Yes,' the alien said gloomily. 'To
escape the disaster ...'

'Silence!' his leader shouted. 'Only
the Ruler will speak with the intruders!'

The aliens pushed them forward into the biggest building, then up another smaller ramp, and finally into a bright chamber. There more aliens were gathered around a taller one, in a splendid robe, seated on a huge chair.

'The Ruler of Ravalle,' muttered the troop leader, as he urged the humans forward. Then he bowed to the seated alien. 'The intruders, my Lord.'

The Ruler waved a hand, and all the other aliens withdrew to the far side of

the room. 'I would have hoped,' the Ruler snarled, glaring at the humans, 'that visitors to Ravalle from other worlds would show respect and friendship. How disappointing that the first ones to arrive should come *now*, for criminal purposes.'

Eldron frowned. 'We're here because your world seemed to be deserted ...'

'Of course,' the Ruler snapped. 'You thought you could rob and plunder our empty lands.'

'We didn't!' Lurah cried.

'I am the Ruler,' the alien sneered, 'and the Ruler is never mistaken. Why else would you come?'

'To investigate,' Eldron said, and quickly explained how the starship had been sent to look into the disappearance of Ravalle's population.

The Ruler snorted. 'Our telescope spotted your little ship as you flew down from the sky. So if your fanciful tale about a mighty starship is intended to frighten me, it has failed.'

'That's not ...' Eldron began.

'Be silent!' the Ruler barked. 'It is *you*, intruder, who should be frightened. We built this underground city, months ago, after my scientists discovered an immense *ball of fire*, the size of a moon, hurtling through space towards us. It will fall into the ocean, *three days* from now – and will destroy most living things on Ravalle!'

'A ball of fire?' Eldron said, astonished. 'Are you sure?'

The Ruler waved a hand. 'I am never mistaken.'

'Perhaps there's something we could do ...' Lurah said.

The Ruler leaned forward, dropping his voice to a croaking whisper. 'You cannot save my land,' he said, 'but you *can* ensure that I and my family will be safe – just in case this city does not withstand the disaster.' He smiled cruelly. 'You can take us into space, in your ship.'

'In the shuttle?' Eldron looked shocked. 'Six is all it can carry ...'

'Perfect,' the Ruler snarled. 'Myself,

the four members of my family, and one of you to fly the thing.'

'No!' Kelsey gasped.

'This is *my* family,' Eldron said fiercely, 'and I won't leave them.'

The Ruler glared. 'Think again, intruder. Otherwise I will chain the three of you *outside* – to take your chances with the fireball.'

'You can't ...!' Eldron raged.

But the Ruler ignored him. 'Take them away,' he called to the troop leader, 'and lock them up. He may change his mind when the disaster grows nearer.'

The troop marched the three humans back down through the building. On a lower level, a long way underground, they were pushed into a small bare room, and the door was closed with a crash.

'Cale will come for us, won't he?' Kelsey asked shakily.

Eldron shook his head. 'Remember, a starship isn't designed to land on a planet.'

Lurah put an arm around Kelsey. 'Don't worry,' she murmured. 'We'll find a way out of this.'

'We'd better,' Kelsey said. 'That Ruler doesn't seem too sure that his underground city is strong enough ...'

'First of all,' Eldron said calmly, 'let's find out about this ball of fire.' And he switched on the comm-link in his collar and called the starship.

Cale was nearly speechless with shock when he heard what had happened. 'What'll you *do*?' he babbled anxiously.

'We'll think of something,' Eldron said. 'But first, use the scanner to see if you can spot something like a huge fireball, heading for Ravalle.'

'Right,' Cale said, and switched off. And for some minutes that seemed like hours to the prisoners, the comm-link remained silent.

At last it hissed into life again. 'Found it!' Cale said excitedly. 'On the far side, so we didn't see it with the planet in the way ... It's heading for the middle of the ocean, and it's very close ... But the aliens calculated wrong – it'll hit in *two* days, not three ...!'

'Cale!' Eldron broke in. 'Tell us what it is!'

'Oh, right,' Cale gulped. 'Sorry. It's a *comet*. It looks huge because it's mostly an enormous cloud of *dust*, around a core of ice – with more dust streaming out like a tail. The aliens think it's a fireball because the dust glows in the sunlight. But it's an ordinary comet.'

'Still, won't that core do lots of damage,' Lurah asked, 'when it hits?'

'Oh, yes,' Cale said. 'The core's not very big – not quite as big as our ship – but it's moving at terrific speed. When it crashes into the ocean there'll be earthquakes and hurricanes – and a tidal wave that might even drown the land mass where you are. So you have to get out!'

'We will,' Eldron said. 'Somehow.' And with a sigh Cale switched off.

'We should have run,' Lurah said gloomily. 'When we first saw them.'

'We might have been shot,' Eldron said. 'Their weapons look like old-style rifles, and our suits wouldn't shield us against bullets.'

Kelsey scowled. 'I wish the starship

had guns. Cale could come and blast this place open.'

'He can't do that,' Eldron said thoughtfully, 'but he *could* come down, whenever they take us out of here. With its deflector shields on, the ship would look like a real fireball, blasting through the atmosphere. That might scare the aliens and distract them, so we could run for the shuttle.'

'It sounds risky,' Lurah murmured.

'We have to try,' Eldron said. 'We can't just sit here.'

But just then, all they could do was sit there as the long endless hours passed. Until, suddenly, the door was flung open.

The troop of aliens stalked in. 'You,' the leader snapped, pointing at Eldron. 'The Ruler will speak with you again.' And before anyone could call Cale or do anything else, Eldron was taken away.

In his high, bright room, the Ruler again glared at Eldron. 'Do you still refuse,' he demanded, 'to fly me and my family into space?'

'Yes,' Eldron said flatly. 'I'm not leaving *my* family.'

The Ruler sneered. 'Stay then. My scientists have been studying your little ship outside, and they believe they can work out how to fly it.'

'They should be careful,' Eldron warned. 'It can be dangerous tinkering with a space-drive ...'

'You are trying to frighten me again, as with your lies about your starship,' the Ruler scoffed. 'But I have faith in my scientists, and I am never mistaken. So I *will* fly to safety – and you intruders will die when the fireball strikes.' With that he waved a hand and Eldron was marched back to the cell.

'I'm going to call Cale and keep him on standby,' Eldron said, after telling Lurah and Kelsey what had happened. 'So he can blast down in a rush, when they come to take us outside. We'll have to be ready to run.'

'We'll be ready,' Lurah promised, and Kelsey nodded.

Eldron switched on his comm-link. 'Cale!' he said urgently. But there was no reply.

Eldron flicked the switch several times and the others tried their comm-links as well. But they heard only a faraway hiss, no reply from Cale.

'What's happened?' Kelsey whispered.

'There may be some interference,' Eldron said. 'I'll keep trying.'

'We're running out of time,' Lurah said. ' We can't be sure how long we have before the comet hits.'

But again, all they could do was sit in silence and wait, with hope fading fast, while more agonising hours passed.

Until at last, once again, they heard the door being unlocked.

'Come on,' Eldron said, as they all leapt up. 'Try to sprint past them before they can shoot ...'

The door opened, and they sprang forward in a frantic charge. But the alien troop, standing back, threw a huge net over them. Its heavy mesh fell around them and held them like thrashing fish.

'The Ruler knew you would try to flee,' the troop leader said. 'The Ruler is never mistaken. Now we will take you outside to meet your fate.'

The troop lifted up the net, with the three humans wrapped in it, and marched out of the building. Eventually they came to the door that led outside. The alien mountains were bathed by a strange lurid light from the comet, looming in the sky like an oversized full moon.

'You can watch it, intruders,' the troop leader said, 'as it falls, tomorrow.'

'Because the scientists were wrong,' one of the other aliens mumbled. 'It is not striking out at sea, but *here*, on top of *us* ...'

'So many of us will die too ...' another alien whimpered.

'Be silent!' the troop leader growled, and led the troop back into the stone building, leaving the three trapped humans staring helplessly up at the comet.

'Don't give up hope,' Lurah said. 'If

Cale makes contact again, I'm sure he'll be able to help us.'

'What if he doesn't?' Kelsey quivered.

'I'm wondering how Cale made the same mistake, thinking the comet was heading for the ocean,' Eldron said quietly. 'It definitely seems to be coming down *here*.'

'Maybe there was a technical glitch on the starship or something,' Lurah said. 'Maybe that's why we can't reach him.'

'I'll try to get a hand free,' Kelsey gasped, wriggling, 'and call him again ...'

But in that moment all their comm-links came to life, and Cale's excited voice burst out. 'I *got* it, I *did* it!' he gabbled. 'It wasn't easy matching the speed, and getting the angle right, and the computers nearly crashed, and I wasn't sure there'd be enough power to fight the speed and the planet's gravity too, but it *worked*, it's *going* ...'

'Cale!' Eldron yelled. 'What are you talking about? Where have you been?'

'Oh, yes, sorry,' Cale gasped. 'I've been using the starship's deflector

shields, with the engines on full power, to push the comet away!'

'Push it?' Kelsey breathed, wide-eyed.

'So that's why it's no longer heading for the ocean!' Lurah said.

'The hard bit was getting it started,' Cale went on. 'But it's turning nicely now. It'll miss the planet by quite a bit. Maybe they'll let you go outside to watch.'

'Oh, we'll be watching,' Eldron said, smiling. 'Thanks, Cale. It was a brilliant idea – you saved us all.'

'But you might have called and *told* us,' Kelsey sniffed.

'I couldn't,' Cale said. 'Being so close to the comet messed up the comm-link. Anyway, are you all right?'

'We will be,' Eldron said. 'And when the comet is safely past, the Ruler might decide to give us our shuttle back.'

Then they lay back in the tangles of the net, keeping the comm-links open, telling Cale what it all looked like as the comet blazed its way across the sky.

Later, the comet's passing stirred up a fierce wind to howl among the mountain peaks, but that soon faded. Then the comet began looking smaller, as it passed by Ravalle and headed off into the trackless depths of space.

A while after that, the door in the stone building opened, and not just the armed troop but the Ruler himself strode out – looking embarrassed and relieved and angry, all at the same time.

'It seems that my scientists made some serious mistakes,' he snapped. 'This vastly expensive underground city was not needed after all. There was never any danger.'

'Actually, there was,' Eldron said quietly. 'But our starship ...'

'Stop!' the Ruler snapped. 'No more fanciful stories about starships. But I *will* get some benefit out of this wretched affair. I will hire *new* scientists, to unravel the secrets of space travel from that small ship of yours. And you three will join my *former* scientists in prison, till I think of what to do with you ...'

He scowled, then, as Eldron spoke into his comm-link. 'Cale,' he said calmly, 'bring the starship down over the building, will you?'

'On my way,' Cale said.

The aliens gaped, astonished by the voice coming from Eldron's collar. Then they stared upwards at the sound of a distant, mighty roar.

Deflector shields aflame as it stormed down into the atmosphere, the starship plunged towards them like a true ball of fire.

The aliens gasped, their eyes filled with terror. And they grew more terrified when the starship slowed, the flames vanished, and its enormous oval shape hovered high above them, silent and ominous.

'Please ...' The Ruler's voice was squeaky. 'Don't let it attack us.'

'It won't,' Eldron said quietly. 'Just set us free, and we'll leave you in peace.'

Frantically the troop unfastened the net, then stood back – glancing fearfully up at the huge hovering ship – as the three humans got to their feet.

'Don't be too hard on those scientists of yours,' Eldron told the Ruler. 'They didn't make a mistake. *You* made the mistake – about us. Remember that, if you ever get more visitors from space.'

'Or more comets,' Kelsey muttered.

Then the three of them turned away, smiling, and walked towards the shuttle waiting nearby.

The Chetty

Myron sat huddled at the back of the arena, sick with worry. 'Let her be all right,' he whispered to himself. 'She *has* to be all right ...'

The arena was inside an enormous building that was a very special zoo. The building held all kinds of creatures from other worlds – large and small, dangerous and harmless, all weirdly *alien*. It had been hugely popular ever since humans had discovered how to travel among the stars and the first 'monsters' were brought back. It became even more popular after some of the creatures had been taught – cruelly, Myron thought – some simple tricks, and made to perform in a twice-weekly show.

For two months, ever since his parents had brought him on his birthday, Myron hadn't missed a show. Twice every week he was there, watching it all, over and over. And hating it.

Myron was a thin, dark-haired twelve-year-old. Wearing the simple one-piece suit and boots that most boys of his age did, he looked fairly ordinary – except that his pale face was twisted with rage and sorrow, as he stared into the arena. There, two creatures like headless hairy sacks on spindly legs were being marched around by their trainer. He jabbed them, often, with an electri-prod – making them squeal, making their heads pop out with startled expressions, making them turn perfect somersaults. The audience howled with laughter, calling for more.

This had been the act Myron's dad had liked best, on that first visit. Myron's parents couldn't begin to understand why Myron hated it so much.

'But they're fantastic creatures from other worlds,' Myron had cried, 'being made to look stupid and clumsy and ugly ...'

'They *are* ugly,' his mother had sniffed.

'And they're being hurt with those prods!' Myron had gone on. 'They must be miserable!'

'You don't know that,' his father had grunted. 'Anyway, who cares? They're just a lot of weird beasts.'

'Monsters,' his mother had snapped.

'They probably don't even feel much,' his father had added. 'And they're better off than if they were dead and stuffed in a museum.'

So Myron had stopped trying to talk to them about it. And after one humiliating time in school, when he had tried to arouse sympathy for the creatures, and the whole class, including

the on-screen teacher, had laughed at him – he hadn't talked to anyone else either.

To make it worse, after that episode in class, the school bully, Jed Felton, and his pals had decided to make him even more of a target. They came to the show often – for a laugh – seldom missing a chance afterwards to pick on Myron.

They were there again that evening, hooting and yelling. But Myron ignored them – because the two somersaulting aliens were being prodded out of the arena, and the presenter's toothy face was filling the overhead screens.

'Now, friends,' he boomed, 'from a world called Chettaran, our last performer, but never our least. She's big, she's bulgy, she's not at all beautiful – everyone's favourite monster, Hetty the chetty!'

Myron leaned forward intently, remembering his incredible shock and delight when he had first seen the chetty.

The big creature had seemed the most amazing of all, with its three thick legs, bulky blue-grey body, domed head, and a tangle of long ropy tentacles around its mouth. But as it had lumbered in, its legs in chains, Myron had looked especially at its large, round, dark eyes. Seeming to see an unbearable depth of suffering in those eyes, Myron's own eyes had blurred with sadness and sympathy. Then, on that first occasion, as the roaring crowd waited for the fun, Myron had gone breathlessly still.

The chetty had *spoken* to him.

Not aloud, but soundlessly, inside his head.

'*Young one*,' the voice had said, '*do you weep for me?*'

The chetty, he had numbly realised, was speaking to his mind – with *its* mind. It wasn't an unthinking monster. It was intelligent – and *telepathic*.

So the strange connection had begun. Now and then, wherever Myron might be, the chetty reached out mentally to him, and talked, most often about its – *her* –

home planet. Although that subject filled her with a desolate grief and longing that soon silenced her.

From then on, Myron attended every show – to offer comfort while the chetty was being prodded painfully through her series of absurd, demeaning tricks. And Myron too felt desolate, at the sight of her being treated as if she was a mindless, unfeeling, clownish beast.

'Chetty, why don't you speak to the trainers?' Myron had once asked. He couldn't manage the alien sounds of her true name, and he wouldn't use the silly name made up by the show's presenter. 'Let them know what you really are ...'

'*I have tried,*' her voice had said in his mind. '*But none can hear. Minds without kindness are closed to me.*'

Myron understood. He knew that most people who enjoyed the shows would be the same – like his parents, or the bullies, or those who had captured the creatures. They were indifferent, even cruel. Kindness wasn't their strong point.

'*Minds can communicate,*' the chetty had once said, '*only when they truly care for others. My world is a place of caring, kindness. Oh, Myron ... my world ...*'

And his eyes had stung again, then, hearing the yearning when she spoke of her home ...

Myron twitched, as around him the crowd's baying grew noisier. And there she was, lumbering slowly into the arena, urged on by two trainers.

Myron's stomach knotted. She looked terrible. Her head was drooping, her skin was a dingy grey without any blueness, and her eyes were watering.

She had seemed ill during the previous show, but this evening she looked worse. The sight twisted Myron's heart, as he waited for her to speak.

'*Myron.*' Her voice was thin, hollow. '*I grow weak, ill.*'

'Do the trainers know?' Myron asked silently, filled with panic. 'Can't someone do something?'

Her inner voice trembled. '*I need special leaves from my world to help me. Without the leaves, there is no hope.*'

Then she stopped, as the prods pushed her into her ludicrous routine – a clumsy chain-jingling dance, balancing on a wobbly see-saw, trying and repeatedly failing to jump through a hoop ...

While the trainers kicked and struck and prodded her, the crowd laughed and laughed. But Myron sat unseeing, despairing, her words echoing within

him – *without the leaves, there is no hope ...*

At last it was over, and the crowd departed as the chetty was driven from the arena. But Myron sat huddled, listening.

'*Myron,*' she said. '*Do not be sad. There is nothing you can do. Only come again ...*'

'I will,' Myron promised silently, from the depths of wretchedness.

A sharp kick on his ankle jolted him painfully into awareness. Jed Felton and his thugs surrounded him, grinning.

'Hey, Kling,' Felton said. It was short for 'weakling', their favourite name for him. 'Stayin' the night?'

'Wants to go and cuddle the monsters,' one of the others chortled.

Myron gritted his teeth and tried to stand up, but Felton shoved him back down, just as a security man strolled up.

'Show's over, lads,' he growled. 'Go and play outside.'

The gang turned away. 'See you outside, Kling,' Felton laughed.

Myron chose another exit, a back door in the immense building. Even so, peering out into the drizzly twilight, he saw the gang lounging nearby, waiting. But they didn't see him as he slipped out and walked the other way.

For a moment a gust of wind turned the drizzle into a squall, and he ducked into a doorway, next to a skip bulging with smelly rubbish. Sheltering there, he wondered if the door was near to where the chetty was kept. But if so, she wasn't aware of him. Probably sleeping, he thought, for she escaped into sleep much of the time, more now that she was ill.

Then as the rain eased, he noticed

a narrow window above the door,
slightly open.

The wild idea seeded itself, grew, and
flowered in the space of a second.

I could sneak in, he thought. Find
the chetty, talk to her, even touch her ...

Then a further flowering of the idea
stopped his breath.

... Even find a way to set her free.

In that quivering moment he heard
footsteps nearby, and hurried away
through the gloom. But the idea blazed
in his mind all the way home, so he
barely noticed his scolding for being
late, or the dinner he ate, or anything
much at all until he was in bed, wide-
eyed in the darkness.

I have to do it, he thought. I could get into all kinds of trouble, and I probably won't be able to get her out, even if I can find her. But I have to try. Because if she's dying ... she shouldn't have to die in chains.

After school the next day he still had no useful ideas, nothing like a plan. Even so, as the late-afternoon shadows darkened, he headed back to the zoo building. But when he reached the door at the back of the building, the disappointment was almost unbearable. The narrow window was shut tight.

It was the same the next day, and the days after that. And in those days he faced another disappointment, for the chetty never spoke to him once. She's *sleeping*, he told himself fiercely, refusing to consider a more dire reason for her silence.

Soon it was the day of the next performance. Instead of buying a ticket, Myron hurried around to the back of the building – and nearly shouted with joy. The window was wide open.

Without pausing to think, he scrambled onto the reeking skip and wriggled through the narrow opening. He found himself in a high-ceilinged, dimly-lit corridor, where sacks lay in untidy heaps. Probably food for the creatures, he thought. I wonder if any of the others are sick ...

From one end of the corridor he faintly heard the false-cheery voice of the show's on-screen presenter and the roaring of the audience. So he went the other way, tense and sweaty, to find where the performing creatures were kept.

A moment later, he dived behind some

bales as a trainer came from the arena,
leading a creature like a tall wingless bird
with spindly legs and an incredibly long
flexible beak. From the other direction
came another trainer, pushing along a
creature with a hard-shelled body, a great
many legs and antennae, and apparently a
head at each end.

The men stopped and chatted, while
Myron held his breath, then they walked
on. The bird-thing was clearly being

returned to where it was kept, so Myron followed carefully.

At last he came to a large doorway marked *Trainers Only*, which opened into a huge dim room. It was filled with cages made of heavy mesh, with the sparkle of a powerful electro-field around them.

While the trainer locked away the bird-thing on the far side, Myron was swiftly creeping in the other direction. He had spotted the chetty.

She was lying on her side, her eyes closed, and Myron wasn't sure that she was breathing.

'Chetty,' he said in a silent whisper. But she didn't move. Panic froze Myron as he heard footsteps coming close, as if the trainer had heard him. But the man went by without looking his way.

Quivering, Myron tried again. 'Chetty!' he said more loudly.

With a wave of relief he saw her eyes slowly open, then fill with wonder as she saw him. '*Myron?*' she said in his mind. '*How have you come here?*'

'I sneaked in,' he said, as the chetty

heaved herself to her feet. She looked even sicker, weaving unsteadily, but hope and joy filled her eyes.

'*Can you free me?*' she cried, the words like bugles in Myron's mind.

Myron didn't reply. He was ducking frantically into the shadows around the side of the cage, as two more trainers came into the room. Seeing nothing suspicious, they headed for a small wall cabinet and opened it. The cabinet had its own light, and Myron saw rows of narrow plastic strips on metal hoops hanging inside. Magno-keys, he thought excitedly.

'Yes,' he murmured to the chetty at last, when the trainers had ambled away. 'I *will* free you.'

He wasn't thinking ahead. He just wanted that key to get her out. Crouching, he crept to the cabinet, found the key with the number of the chetty's cage, and crept back.

When the magno-key slid into its slot, the electro-field shut down and the whole front of the cage slid upwards.

The chetty's jubilation washed over
Myron's mind.

    'Outside, Myron,' she said pleadingly.
'I must be outside.'

'Yes,' Myron said, finding that the key unlocked the chains as well. 'Sshhh,' he added, as the chetty flung the chains from her tentacles with a rattling clank. But no one else heard, for a trainer had brought back the two-headed creature which was hissing shrilly. And no one looked their way, for another trainer was taking out the next performer – a shiny-red thing like an enormously thick snake.

As they left the room, there was no one else in sight. Myron patted the chetty's leg, which felt like a tree-stump covered in soft, warm leather. 'Follow me,' he told her. 'Be ready to hide if someone comes ...' And they simply walked out into the corridor, seeing only the trainer and the red 'snake' well ahead.

In a few tense minutes, Myron was unbolting and opening the narrow door below the window where he had entered. The chetty was still swaying with illness and weakness, but her tentacles lifted, quivering, as if reaching out for freedom.

'Wait, Chetty,' Myron said. 'I'll make sure there's no one around.'

Leaving her in the doorway, he crept out along the twilit street, peering around, hardly able to believe it had been so easy. But he knew the hard part was to come – looking after a fugitive, dying, alien creature. I'll find a place to hide her, he told himself. And I'll stay with her till ... till the end.

Seeing no one, he turned to go back – and shock hit him like a sledgehammer.

The doorway was empty. The chetty had gone.

It couldn't have been trainers, he thought numbly. They would have made noise – and the door's still open. She's wandered off, he thought, looking wildly around. But where? And *why*?

Myron dashed to the corner of the

building, but saw only another quiet street, with strolling people who didn't look as if they'd just seen an alien creature. Panting, he sprinted to the other corner, but again saw an ordinary street and some people – including five people he badly didn't want to see.

'Hey there, Kling!' Jed Felton and his thugs were swarming around before Myron could escape. 'Why're you flappin' around back here, aren't you watching the show?'

'Maybe wormin' in the bins,' one said, and the others laughed.

'Maybe creepin' clear of us,' Felton sneered. 'Like last time.'

'Not clear now,' another snickered, as Felton grabbed Myron's arm.

Myron struggled, but it was no use. It was their favourite game – pushing him roughly from one to another, waiting for him to stumble and fall, or finally tripping him, and then the kicking ...

But when he stiffened, staring past his enemies, his eyes widening, the bullies automatically turned to see what

he was seeing. And screamed.

The chetty loomed over them, looking strong, healthy, restored … and furious.

The bullies howled again as five of her tentacles coiled around their necks, jerking them towards her.

Then they all disappeared.

Myron almost collapsed with shock, reeling back against the building, then gasped when the chetty reappeared in front of him.

'*Myron,*' her inner voice murmured. '*Kindest one, see how you have saved me.*'

'What … ?' Myron choked. 'Where … ? Where did you go? How did you do that?'

'*With my mind,*' the chetty said. '*We speak with our minds, my kind, and we move by them. Our minds carry us where we wish, one leap, any distance. I went to my world, Myron, for the leaves to heal me.*'

'You just *went*? To your *planet*?' Myron gulped, dazed. 'But – but – if you could do that, why stay in a cage? Why let them even *capture* you?'

'*I was trapped with a sleep-dart,*' the chetty said sadly, '*and I woke in chains, in a cage, unable to escape. I must be in the open air and free, for the mind leap.*'

Myron felt a new sadness, realising how terrible it must have been for the chetty in captivity.

'What did you do with the boys, Chetty?'

'*Left them in my world,*' the chetty said, '*in terror. I shall return them soon.*'

Terror, Myron thought. Good. 'What's terrifying them?' he asked.

'*Only strangeness,*' the chetty said. '*Nothing harmful. See.*'

A tentacle wrapped gently round him, and suddenly they were on a mossy slope, in warm sunlight under a yellow sky. A breeze carried spicy scents from patches of orange-leaved bushes, on which other chetties were feeding in the distance.

'It's beautiful,' Myron breathed. 'And so quiet.'

'*It is a peaceful world,*' the chetty agreed. '*Not as your world, with its anger and cruelty and noise. Yet it is your place, Myron. You must be there, I here.*'

Instantly they were on the quiet twilit street again.

'Will I ever see you again?' Myron asked, upset.

'*Often,*' the chetty assured him. '*When I have spent time with my loved ones, I will visit, or carry you to my world for a visit.*'

Myron sighed happily. Then an idea struck him.

'Chetty,' he said thoughtfully, 'if you can move around so easily, we could set those other creatures free. You could take them back to their worlds.'

'*I cannot travel somewhere,*' the chetty said, '*without first knowing where it is.*'

Myron frowned, then brightened. 'I could find out what planets they're from, on the Datastream!'

'*It is a kind thought,*' the chetty said, her eyes warm, '*and since we are bound together, Myron, who knows what we might be abe to do?*'

Then she vanished again, leaving Myron smiling in the darkened street.